Charlie

Based on
The Railway Series
by the
Rev. W. Awdry

Illustrations by
Robin Davies
and **Nigel Chilvers**

EGMONT

EGMONT

We bring stories to life

First published in Great Britain in 2017
by Egmont UK Limited
The Yellow Building, 1 Nicholas Road, London W11 4AN

Thomas the Tank Engine & Friends™

CREATED BY BRITT ALLCROFT

HiT entertainment

ISBN 978 1 4052 8574 2
66189/1
Printed in Italy

Written by Emily Stead. Designed by Claire Yeo.
Series designed by Martin Aggett.

FSC
MIX
Paper
FSC® C018306

Egmont is passionate about helping to preserve the world's remaining ancient forests.
We only use paper from legal and sustainable forest sources.

This book is made from paper certified by the Forestry Stewardship Council® (FSC®),
an organisation dedicated to promoting responsible management of forest resources.
For more information on the FSC, please visit www.fsc.org. To learn more about Egmont's
sustainable paper policy, please visit www.egmont.co.uk/ethical

When a new engine arrived
from the Mainland, he was so
much fun! I wanted Charlie to think
I was fun, too! But sometimes
it's more important to
be Really Useful . . .

At the Washdown one day, Thomas had some exciting news.

"I have a **special** passenger today," he puffed to Percy. "I'm collecting Alicia Botti, the famous singer, from the Docks and taking her to the Town Hall for her concert."

Percy smiled. "Someone else is arriving at the Docks today, too," he told his friend.

"Who is it?" asked Thomas.

"A new engine called Charlie," said Percy. "Everyone says he's the most **fun** engine ever, even more **fun** than you!"

And Percy chuffed cheerfully away.

"Cinders and ashes!" said Thomas, as he set off for the Docks. "Could any engine be more fun than me?"

Thomas smiled proudly as he saw Alicia Botti waiting to meet him. Then he spotted a small purple engine.

"That must be Charlie," Thomas peeped.

"He's very **small**, and he doesn't look much **fun**," Thomas whispered to his carriages.

The purple engine puffed up beside Thomas. "Hello, I'm Charlie," he smiled. "Are you Thomas? The Mainland engines say that you're even more fun than me!"

Thomas was surprised!

Just then, The Fat Controller arrived.
"It's Charlie's first day today," he boomed.
"Will you look after him, Thomas?"

"Yes, Sir," Thomas replied.

Cheeky Charlie blew his whistle loudly, **"Peeep!"**

"Let's race to the Dairy!" Charlie chirped.

"I'm too busy to race today," said Thomas.

Charlie frowned. "I thought you were a **fun** engine. But you're not **fun** at all!"

This made Thomas cross, so he agreed to a race. "I'll take Miss Botti to the Town Hall afterwards," he said.

The race was on! Thomas and Charlie **thundered** through tunnels and **steamed** through stations. Thomas beat Charlie to the Dairy by a buffer, and Alicia Botti sang all the way there!

"Let's race to Knapford next," Charlie smiled.

Thomas was late, but he didn't want Charlie to think he wasn't fun. "One last race," he agreed.

But Thomas' Driver said it was time to go.
Thomas said goodbye to Charlie and sped away.

As Thomas bumped onto a bridge, his coupling
hook went **SNAP!** His carriages uncoupled, but
Thomas didn't notice!

"Where is Miss Botti?" The Fat Controller boomed,
as Thomas arrived at the station.

Thomas felt terrible.

Thomas puffed back the way he had come. He met Charlie at a junction and told him the problem.

"Let's race to your carriages," Charlie chuffed. "The winner will be the Number 1 **Fun** Engine!"

"No, Charlie," said Thomas. "Being Really Useful is more important than being fun."

The signal changed, and Thomas steamed away.

Thomas' wheels whirred with worry. Where had he left his carriages? Then he heard someone singing — it was Alicia Botti! A crowd of people had gathered to listen to her.

Thomas puffed backwards slowly. Then an Engineer fixed the coupling rod.

"I'm sorry I left you behind, Miss Botti," said Thomas. "But it's time to go."

Everyone was waiting at the Town Hall Station when Thomas puffed in with Annie and Clarabel.

"You've made Miss Botti very late, Thomas," said The Fat Controller crossly.

But Alicia Botti wasn't angry. "I've had such **fun** with Thomas!" she smiled.

"Peep! Peep!" Thomas whistled in delight. And his fun friend, Charlie, joined in too.

More about Charlie

whistle

lamp

cab

nameplate

buffer

coupling hook

Charlie's challenge to you

Look back through the pages of this book
and see if you can spot:

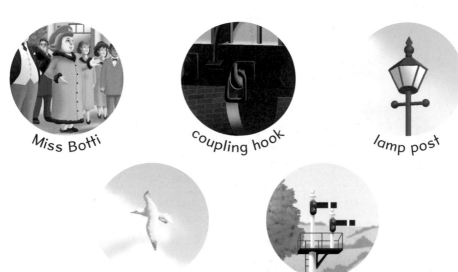

Miss Botti

coupling hook

lamp post

seagull

signals

THE THOMAS ENGINE ADVENTURES

From Thomas to Harold the Helicopter, there is an Engine Adventure to thrill every Thomas fan.

 Thomas
 Percy
 Harold
 James
 Cranky
 Spencer

 Gordon
 Flynn
 Toby
 Henry
 Hiro
 Emily

 Thomas and Bertie's Race
 Thomas Goes Crash!
 Kevin
 Diesel
 Troublesome Trucks
 Charlie

EGMONT